BECCI MURR

GRANNY PUT A Pumpkin ON HER NOGGIN

well stuck →

A Granny Book

www.llamahousebooks.com

For Harry Edmondson,
the world's greatest Granny fan
xx

ISBN: 978-1-913944-38-4

Published by Llama House Children's Books

Granny put a **PUMPKIN** on her noggin.

Told you it would fit! she proudly said.

proper chuffed

Mother laughed so hard she started sobbing,
Till Granny tried to lift it from her head...

I cannot get this pumpkin off my noggin!

Now everyone will stare at me all night.

I shoved my bonce right in,

And it wedged beneath my chin,

Oh, won't someone hide this pumpkin out of sight?

well
stuck

3

Grandpa eyed the ceiling in the hall.

This lamp-shade will disguise your scary head!

Frankenstein's grandpa →

4

He took a light-up skull from off the wall,
And placed it into Granny's mouth instead...

I cannot get this pumpkin off my noggin!

Now everyone will stare at me all night.

My head's a *human-light*,

But your grandpa's not so bright,

Oh, won't someone hide this pumpkin out of sight?

Mother tried another plan instead.

My make-up kit will have you looking ace!

Mrs Broccoli-Hair

She took the Halloween wig off her head,
Then smeared some lippy onto Granny's face...

I cannot get this pumpkin off my noggin!

Now everyone will stare at me all night.

I'm still insanely scary,

Plus, I look like Cousin Mary,

Oh, won't someone hide this pumpkin out of sight?

Cousin Mary

11

Father snatched the cloth from off the table.

Let's make you look like furniture! he cried.

battier than ever

He flung the sheet as high as he was able,
Then grabbed a vase of flowers from the side...

I cannot get this pumpkin off my noggin!

Now everyone will stare at me all night.

This vase is overflowing,

And I can't see where I'm going,

Oh, won't someone hide this pumpkin out of sight?

Auntie quickly leapt up from her seat.

I know the perfect place where you'll blend in!

banana
horns

She ushered Granny out into the street,
Then eyed the zebra-crossing with a grin...

Auntie's REAL feet

17

I cannot get this pumpkin off my noggin!

Now everyone will stare at me all night.

A dog wee-ed on your shoe,

And I think I need one too,

Oh, won't someone hide this pumpkin out of sight?

19

But when he asked his friend to come inside...

I cannot get this pumpkin off my noggin!

Now everyone will stare at me all night.

I bet you never knew,

That your granny does Kung Fu,

Oh, won't someone hide this pumpkin out of sight?

25

Everyone went

FULLY LOOP-THE-LOOP!

Mum's disco-face

Dad hung around while Mum danced on a stool,

And just as Grandpa tipped the pumpkin soup,

I shouted...

gloopy soupy

27

Granny's head looks really cool!

29

We've all got silly pumpkins on our noggins!

Our heads look daft but we don't care at all.

You never need to hide,

With your family by your side,

But...

31

MORE GRANNY BOOKS...
COLLECT THEM ALL!

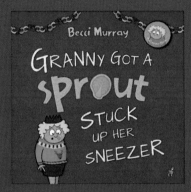

Becci Murray

GRANNY GOT A **sprout** STUCK UP HER SNEEZER

Becci Murray

GRANNY DROPPED HER **chompers** DOWN THE TOILET

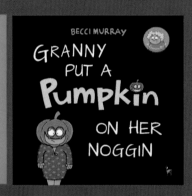

BECCI MURRAY

GRANNY PUT A **Pumpkin** ON HER NOGGIN

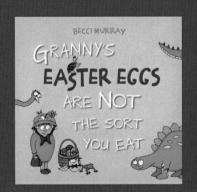

BECCI MURRAY

GRANNY'S EASTER EGGS ARE NOT THE SORT YOU EAT

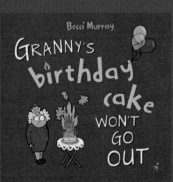

Becci Murray

GRANNY'S **birthday** cake WON'T GO OUT

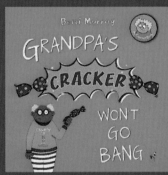

Becci Murray

GRANDPA'S **CRACKER** WON'T GO BANG

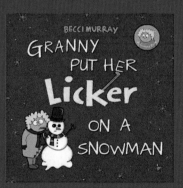

BECCI MURRAY

GRANNY PUT HER **Licker** ON A SNOWMAN

www.llamahousebooks.com

From the author and illustrator of the Granny books...

UNICORN ISLAND

series one stars the unicorns of Munch Town →

Explore the new illustrated chapter book series for ages 4 - 8 years!

Becci Murray is a mum and proudly independent author and illustrator from the UK. She previously wrote for children's television and is the creator of the bestselling 'Granny' book series.

If you enjoyed reading 'Granny Put a Pumpkin on Her Noggin', please consider leaving a review wherever you purchased the book to help other young readers discover the story.

Manufactured by Amazon.ca
Acheson, AB